First U.S. edition 2011

Library of Congress Cataloging-in-Publication Data

James, Simon, date.
George flies south / Simon James. — 1st U.S. ed.
p. cm.
Summary: George does not feel ready to learn to fly, leave his nest,
and go south with the other birds, despite his mother's encouragement,
but when a strong autumn wind gets hold of the nest, he may have no choice.
ISBN 978-0-7636-5724-6
[1. Birds — Fiction. 2. Animals — Infancy — Fiction.
3. Flight — Fiction. 4. Nests — Fiction.] I. Title.
PZ7.J1544Geo 2011
[E] — dc22   2010049468

11 12 13 14 15 16 SCP 10 9 8 7 6 5 4 3 2 1

Printed in Humen, Dongguan, China

This book was typeset in Goudy.
The illustrations were done in ink and watercolor.

Candlewick Press
99 Dover Street
Somerville, Massachusetts 02144

visit us at www.candlewick.com

CANDLEWICK PRESS

Simon James

George Flies South

The leaves on the
trees were turning brown.
Winter was coming.

Lots of birds were heading south.

It was time for George to learn to fly.

"Are you ready, George?" said his mom.

"Not quite," said

George.

"I might fall."

"I think I like my nest best."

"Will you get some worms, Mom?"

"I'll stay here."

While George waited, a strong gust of wind

swept through the park.

It tore through the branches,

scattering the leaves everywhere.

George's nest wobbled . . .

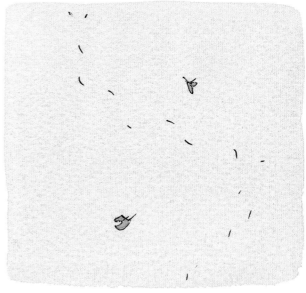

and lifted
into the air.

"Look, Mom!"
said George.
"Look at me!"

"I'm flying!

Wheee!"

But George's mom was too far away.

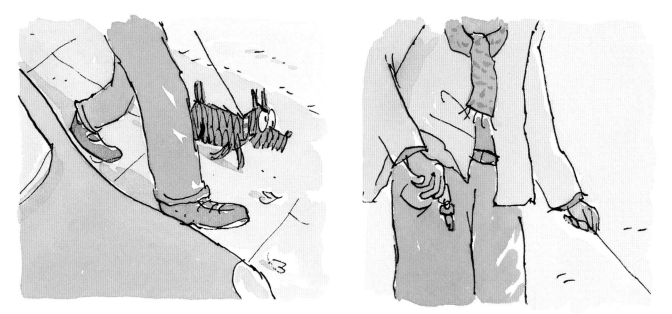

She couldn't hear him calling.

When she flew back, George and his nest were gone!

"George! George!" she cried. "Where are you?"

"I'm here, Mom!" called George. "I flew down in my nest!"

Then, without warning,

George and his nest were on the move again.

"Am I going

south, Mom?"

asked George.

"Hold on!" shouted his mom. "I'm coming!"

But George couldn't hold on,

and his nest took off into the air.

"Look at me, Mom!

Look at me!" said George.

"I'm flying again!"

"You can't stay here, George," said his mom.

"You've got to leave your nest. Try to flap your wings!"

George tried.   "Try harder!"

"What are
we going to
do, Mom?"

Finally the boat stopped. George was lifted

up, up, up into the air.

"Don't move,

George!"

said his mom.

George looked down.

He was glad he still had his nest.

"Don't worry," said his mom. We'll try again tomorrow."

George curled up and fell fast asleep.

The next morning, George woke with a start.

"Look out, George!"

shouted his mom.

CRACK! The cat landed,

and George's nest began to fall.

"Don't worry,
Mom. I'm all right,"
shouted George.

Down, down, down, he fell.

Twig by twig, the nest fell apart

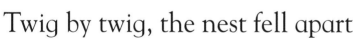

until only George was left!

"Mom!"

cried George.

"I've lost my nest!"

"George, you have
to flap your wings,"
shouted his mom.
"Now! It's time."

George tried
really hard.

"You can do it,"
said his mom.
"I'm trying,"
said George, and
with a deep breath
and a huge beat
of his wings . . .

George flew!

"I knew you could do it, George,"

said his mom.

"I'm ready to fly south now!"

said George. "Let's go! I hope

there's lots of worms . . ."